Dear Parent:

Congratulations! Your child is taking the first steps on an exciting journey. The destination? Independent reading!

STEP INTO READING® will help your child get there. The program offers five steps to reading success. Each step includes fun stories and colorful art. There are also Step into Reading Sticker Books, Step into Reading Math Readers, Step into Reading Write-In Readers, Step into Reading Phonics Readers, and Step into Reading Phonics First Steps! Boxed Sets—a complete literacy program with something for every child.

Learning to Read, Step by Step!

Ready to Read Preschool–Kindergarten
• big type and easy words • rhyme and rhythm • picture clues
For children who know the alphabet and are eager to begin reading.

Reading with Help Preschool–Grade 1
• basic vocabulary • short sentences • simple stories
For children who recognize familiar words and sound out new words with help.

Reading on Your Own Grades 1–3
• engaging characters • easy-to-follow plots • popular topics
For children who are ready to read on their own.

Reading Paragraphs Grades 2–3
• challenging vocabulary • short paragraphs • exciting stories
For newly independent readers who read simple sentences with confidence.

Ready for Chapters Grades 2–4
• chapters • longer paragraphs • full-color art
For children who want to take the plunge into chapter books but still like colorful pictures.

STEP INTO READING® is designed to give every child a successful reading experience. The grade levels are only guides. Children can progress through the steps at their own speed, developing confidence in their reading, no matter what their grade.

Remember, a lifetime love of reading starts with a single step!

THIS BOOK IS A GIFT
OF FRIENDS
OF THE ORINDA LIBRARY

Special thanks to Vicki Jaeger, Monica Okazaki, Lauren Boyle, Christine Chang, Rob Hudnut, Tiffany J. Shuttleworth, Tulin Ulkutay, Ayse Ulkutay, Luke Carroll, Lil Reichmann, Cherish Bryck, Andrea Schimpl, and Walter P. Martishius

Visit us on the Web!
www.stepintoreading.com
www.barbie.com

Educators and librarians, for a variety of teaching tools, visit us at
www.randomhouse.com/teachers

Library of Congress Cataloging-in-Publication Data
Landolf, Diane Wright.
Barbie Thumbelina / adapted by Diane Wright Landolf ; based on the original screenplay by Elise Allen. — 1st ed.
    p. cm. — (Step into reading. Step 2)
ISBN 978-0-375-85690-7 (trade) — ISBN 978-0-375-95690-4 (lib. bdg.)
I. Barbie Thumbelina (Motion picture) II. Title. III. Title: Thumbelina.
PZ7.L2317345Bar 2009 [E]—dc22 2008028991

Printed in the United States of America

10 9 8 7 6 5

First Edition

Barbie™ Thumbelina

Adapted by Diane Wright Landolf

Based on the original screenplay by Elise Allen

Illustrated by Ulkutay Design Group and Allan Choi

Random House 🏠 New York

Thumbelina is tiny.

She made wings.

Her best friends,

Chrysella and Janessa,

watch her fly!

They are Twillerbees.
They all live
in a big field.

The three friends
try out their wings.
Then they hear a
rumble.

It is humans!
Humans are coming
with their big trucks.

In one truck
rides a spoiled girl
named Makena.
"I want those flowers,"
she tells her parents.

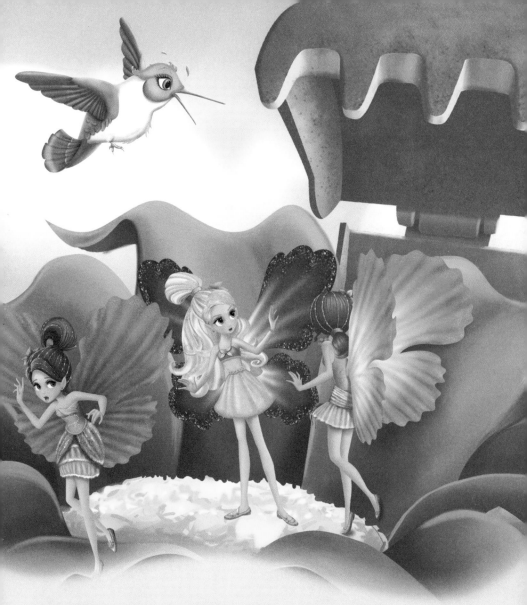

As the friends watch,
a bulldozer comes close.
They need to hide!

When they come out,
they are in
a huge bedroom.
It is Makena's room.

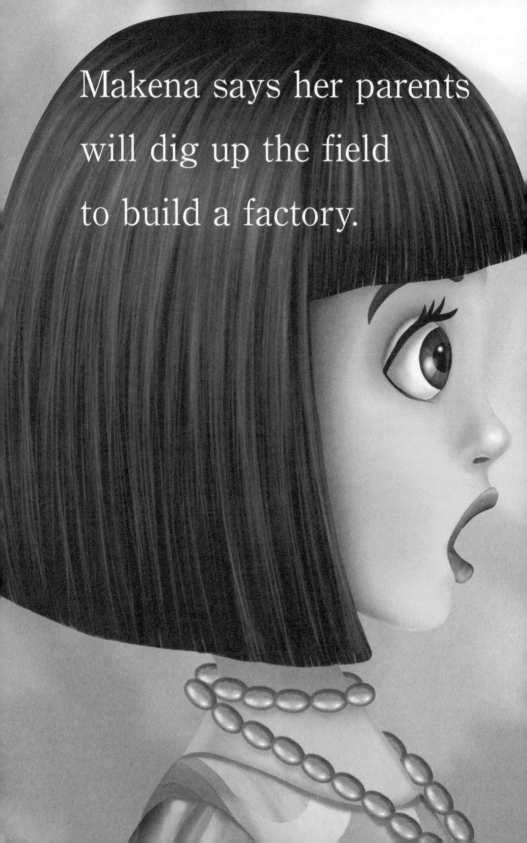

Makena says her parents
will dig up the field
to build a factory.

Thumbelina is angry.

Chrysella and Janessa

fly back to the field

to warn the others.

Thumbelina stays.
She wants to try to stop
Makena's parents.

At the field,
Twillerbees work hard.
They use their magic
to make vines grow
all over the trucks!

The field is safe
for one more day.

Thumbelina asks Makena
to help save the field.
Makena agrees.

She asks her parents
not to build the factory.
They love Makena,
but they are busy.
They do not listen to her.

Thumbelina finds
an old drawing.

It shows Makena's family.

Later, Makena gives
Thumbelina a makeover.
Now they are
best friends.

Thumbelina makes
a garden for her friend.

It is just like the one
in the drawing.
Makena loves it.

Then Makena's
friend Violet comes over.
Thumbelina thinks
Makena just wants
to show her off.

Her feelings are hurt.
She flies home.

Makena bikes
to Twillerbee Field.

She says Thumbelina
is her only true friend.
She wants to help
save the field.
Thumbelina has a plan.

At Makena's house,
the Twillerbees make
the garden even better.

Makena leads her parents
to the garden.
She tells them
about the Twillerbees.
This time, they listen.

The family rushes
to the field.
Makena stands
in front of the trucks!

The work stops.
The field is safe.

The new friends enjoy
the field together.
It is a perfect day
for a picnic!